KIDNAP

at the

Catfish Cafe

THE ADVENTURES OF Minnie and Max

KIDNAP at the Catfish Cafe

Patricia Reilly Giff
illustrated by
Lynne Cravath

SCHOLASTIC INC.

New York Toronto London Auckland Sydney
Mexico City New Delhi Hong Kong

For Vincent Ambrose,
Inspector, NYPD,
in living memory

ISBN 0-439-17922-X

Text copyright © 1998 by Patricia Reilly Giff.
Illustrations copyright © 1998 by Lynne Cravath.
All rights reserved.
Published by Scholastic Inc., 555 Broadway, New York, NY 10012,
by arrangement with Viking Children's Books,
a division of Penguin Putnam Inc.
SCHOLASTIC and associated logos are trademarks and/or
registered trademarks of Scholastic Inc.

12 11 10 9 8 7 6 5 4   2 3 4 5/0

Printed in the U.S.A.   40

First Scholastic printing, March 2000

Set in Sabon

CONTENTS

CAT

Max was a drop-in. He dropped into my life one summer day, nearly killing himself doing it. He was all skin and bones, and filthy, all meow, with a look that said, "How about a handout? I'll take anything."

That was at first.

That was when he was grateful for a salty little sardine, a scratch under his chin, and a quick nap on my bunched-up sweater.

That lasted for about an hour.

Then he made his real move. On me, Minnie. On my brother Orlando's kitchen. And mostly on my detective business.

I have to tell you, the detective business wasn't so hot anyway. No calls, no emergencies, no cases. Maybe it was because I had set it up only two days ago. That was after my U FISH I'LL ROW business hadn't worked out. Neither had SEE SHARKFIN BAY—ONE HOUR—ONE BUCK. And MINNIE'S MINING FOR GOLD COMPANY had been a disaster.

But I always needed money. I needed something to do.

Well, I certainly found something. I should say *we*. Max and me. Maybe I should begin at the beginning, tell about saving Max, tell about the Klutz, and the kid, and the kidnapping. Tell about the whole thing.

KLUTZ

It was early on Monday. I was sitting under pier twelve at Emmons Avenue, having breakfast: a couple of sardines on a Portuguese roll. I felt good; actually, I felt great. It was summer, so I didn't have to think about school or bother with homework.

Right now, I had a crab's-eye view of Sharkfin Bay. First I watched *The Sea Dragon* speed out with a fishing party. Then *My Own Gypsy*, a red wreck of a tugboat, headed for deep water.

Across the street, opposite the pier, my brother Orlando was setting tables for the outdoor luncheon at the CATFISH CAFE, SUPER SOUTHERN COOKING. If you'd asked me I would have said, Why bother? Four customers might show up. If Orlando was lucky. The only thing he knew about Southern cooking was that he had been born in Florida. His Southern dishes were filled with canned peaches and chopped walnuts with teeth-cracking shells mixed in.

Anyway I was sitting there thinking about this and that,

listening to the lap of the water under the pier. I could smell low tide and kerosene from the boats. I was feeling a little guilty that I wasn't helping Orlando. I ducked my head. If Orlando saw me I'd be back in the kitchen in two seconds, washing dishes. Just because he was twelve years older than me, Orlando thought he was my father.

Just then the Klutz appeared out of nowhere. A grown-up klutz.

Her eyeglasses were sliding down her nose. Her blond hair was dangling in her eyes. She skittered down the next pier with a can of worms under one arm and a fishing rod under the other. She was wearing lace-up shoes. Lace-ups to go fishing? I sat back against the damp steps, watching. Then her feet went out from under her and the can of worms went flying.

The worms were probably thrilled. They plopped off the pier and into the water, free.

I was ready to get up and help her, when a truck rattled up the avenue. Music blared from the front. LUMBER JACK was painted on the side. Boards hung off the back with a red warning flag. And there was a cat. He was holding onto a board, claws dug in, ears flat against his head. He looked scared. No, he looked spitting mad. I was the one who was scared. The cat was going to use up one of his nine lives any second. I flew up the steps barefoot, my heart pounding.

The cat was in luck. The light turned red. The truck slowed down and stopped. By that time I was halfway to the street, circling a fisherman with a pail of porgies.

I could see the cat prying at something between the boards with one dirty paw. Whatever it was popped loose. He darted after it along the board, rolling it like a ball.

All the time I was yelling, trying to get the driver's attention. Then the light changed and the truck began to move. The cat's toy bounced off the back. He stared after it with yellow eyes, tail up, paw out.

And then, even though I had never seen that skinny, miserable-looking cat before, I knew what he was going to do. I raced toward the truck, reaching up, reaching higher, as the cat jumped . . .

. . . and landed in my arms.

Never mind that he was digging into my skin as hard as he had dug into the boards. Never mind that I had stubbed both big toes on the curb getting back off the street.

He was safe. And so was I. Orlando was plunking plates down next to the forks on the tables and hadn't even seen what was going on. The Klutz wasn't paying attention. I could see her, hair over her eyes, fooling around with her fishing rod.

Back under the ladder, I scooped up my breakfast and slid down onto a wooden raft that was tied to a piling. I took the last salty sardine from the Portuguese roll and laid it out for the cat. It wouldn't be enough. I'd have to make a pass around the back door of the Catfish Cafe later for something else, maybe a slab of mackerel slathered with peaches. I'd have to go back soon anyway. Fold napkins. Sweep the bread crumbs from under the tables.

Actually, Orlando wasn't paying attention to napkins and bread crumbs these days. He was waiting for a special customer. A redhead.

"She was here just once," he had said. "She loved my steamed clams. She loved my bluefish. She said she loves to cook. I know she'll be back." He had smoothed his mustache, thinking. "She even dumped the chickpeas into the peach fries. A new recipe. I think it will be the Monday special from now on."

The cat devoured the sardine, his own Monday special. Then he rubbed his wiry body against my legs. I reached down and ran my fingers over his rough back. I could hear the growl of his purring as he settled himself down for a nap.

I don't know what made me look back toward the street. I don't know why I wanted to see what the cat had been playing with. But then I saw the glint of it, the marble shape. I headed up toward the thing in the street, keeping one eye on it. I kept the other eye on the Catfish Cafe, which now had one customer, Mrs. Vorr.

I waited until Orlando, tray held high, went back inside the kitchen. Then I made a mad dash across Emmons Avenue, scooped the thing up, and threw myself back down under the pier. "Not bad, Max," I told the cat, picking a name for him on the spot. He looked up at me.

"I'm Minnie," I said. Then I opened my hand.

I couldn't believe what I was looking at.

I just couldn't believe it.

3

CATFISH CAFE

A ring. It was gorgeous, with silver curlicues. In the middle was a piece of amber. It was the color of—I tried to think. *Rich, golden honey,* one cereal ad said. Yes.

Anyone who hung around Sharkfin Bay long enough knew about amber, and Orlando and I had lived there for as long as I could remember. After my mom and dad died, we lived with Bird Berry, Orlando's friend. But then Orlando grew tall, grew gorgeous, grew a mustache. Suddenly he was old enough to run a restaurant, and run me, too. And Bird Berry had gone away to Muck Island to raise pigeons.

Sometimes I thought about my mother. "Just like you, Minnie," Orlando had said. "Off and running every minute." And I thought about my father. "Just like Orlando, mustache and all," Bird Berry had said. But it was so long ago I could hardly remember them at all.

I held up the ring now, staring at the amber with one eye.

The whole world looked like marmalade. Amber was from far away, from around the Baltic Sea. And many of the people in Sharkfin Bay came from there. Everyone seemed to have two or three pieces of amber.

I turned it in my hand. I loved the feel of it. I loved the feeling of the sun. I closed my eyes.

I woke thinking that someone was watching. It was Max. Awake. Staring at me. I stared back. I could see it. He wanted a chunk of chicken, a slab of salmon, a slice of sausage. He was starving.

I hoisted him up to my shoulder, feeling him rub his pointy chin against my cheek. I jammed the amber ring into my jeans pocket and my sneakers onto my feet, and headed for the Catfish Cafe.

Lunch was over now. Orlando would be taking a nap in our rowboat, *The Crab's Legs*. Perfect. I'd dump the dishes in the dishwasher. I'd sweep the floor. Max could have a shrimp feast on his own. I popped one into my mouth as I passed the bowl to Max a few minutes later.

Then I set to work. Orlando would think he was in heaven. I left the sink shining and the floor spotless. All the time I was thinking Max and I were rich. The amber ring was in my pocket, gleaming, glowing. It had dollar signs in neon lights.

There were a million things I could do with the money after I sold the ring to one of the pawn shops along the avenue. The most important thing was to get Orlando's restaurant going. We could hire a real cook, not one who spooned peaches over everything. . . .

But wait a minute. Amber might be rolling around on the shores of the Baltic Sea all by itself, but not on the shores of Sharkfin Bay. That amber ring belonged to someone.

I reached around Max and took another teeny shrimp. In back of me, the kitchen door banged open. Orlando stood there, hands on his hips. He pointed one long finger at Max. "Is that a cat? I can't believe there's a cat in my kitchen."

Orlando could be pretty dramatic when he wanted to.

"Out." His droopy mustache quivered.

I slapped my forehead. I could be dramatic, too. "No," I said. "It's a panther from the African rain forest."

Orlando usually laughed at stuff like that. But this time he closed his eyes. "When I open them," he told me, "I don't want to see that cat. Ever again."

"How was Max supposed to know he didn't belong on the counter?" I asked. "How could he know he shouldn't eat that shrimp?"

"Shrimp?" Orlando looked at the empty bowl on the counter. "Twenty-five shrimp? Enough for five customers."

I wanted to say we never had five customers, but I didn't think it was a good idea.

"Take that cat back," Orlando said.

"I don't know where . . ."

He shook his head. "No, Minnie. I can't run a restaurant, take care of you, *and* have a cat."

By this time Max was under the table, peering out at Orlando as if he had lost his mind.

"Please." My throat was tight. "I've never had a cat. Besides, I know what this cat is thinking."

For a moment Orlando looked sad for me. Then he shook his head. "Too bad you didn't know what he was eating." He dropped the empty shrimp bowl into the sink.

"He was starving," I said. "It won't happen anymore."

Orlando's mustache looked as if it was in a thunderstorm.

I bit my lip. "Come on, Max."

Max slid out from under the table, one eye on Orlando, and followed me outside. I plunked myself down on the dock across the street. Max plunked himself down on my lap.

We sat there watching the fishing boats chugging back with sunburned fishermen and holds filled with bluefish. We listened as the fishermen began to call, "Get your fresh fish he-ah!"

The seagulls swooped in, ready to fight for scraps of bait and fishheads. And I was trying to figure out what to do. Max and I belonged together. I knew that.

I ran my hand over the knobs on his bony back. I could see a couple of snow-white hairs on his neck. He looked better to me already after a little food. His coat was beginning to shine.

"What can we do?" I whispered.

Max didn't answer. Of course he didn't. He stared at me with Life-Saver yellow eyes.

I kept twisting it around in my mind. Suppose I set up a spot for him under the pier? I could get a box and line it with my old bathrobe. I could bring food down to him.

But what about next winter? The steps would be slippery and icy cold with the mist coming up off the bay. I could almost see Max shivering on the raft.

No. He had to have a home.

Then something else popped into my head. Suppose he belonged to someone? Suppose he had gotten lost?

I had to find out. Maybe the person who owned him would let me come to visit. The lump in my throat was as big as the amber ring in my pocket. And that reminded me. I had to find out who owned the amber ring.

Then I thought of something else. I had found a mystery.

Actually, I had found two mysteries.

I was in business.

4

CLUBHOUSE

It was steamy hot, and the pier was crowded. Half the people in Sharkfin Bay were there to buy fresh flounder for supper. The other half were trying to catch their own.

I sat down on a bench. I wanted to think. Max wanted to play. He was standing on my shoulder trying to capture my ponytail.

"We have to find out where you belong," I said.

Max lunged.

"Ouch," I said. I had to start with the truck. I tried to remember everything I had seen.

"Too bad you can't talk," I told Max. "We'd find that truck in a minute."

Max frowned at me, actually frowned. I could see a tiny line between those yellow eyes. It seemed as if his whiskers bristled.

I frowned, too, trying to remember. "It was a flatbed truck. Green, wasn't it?"

Max looked at the water. So did I. It was smooth as silk.

The gulls sitting on the posts were reflected in the bay.

I closed my eyes. "Red flag dangling off the end. *Lumber Jack* written on the side. I think I've seen it at the garage."

In front of me someone was reeling in a fish. I could see its silvery body arching. I could see the fisherman leaning over.

The fisherman. Blond hair dangling over her eyes, glasses sliding down her nose. The Klutz? She had caught a fish?

But no. The fish gave an enormous leap. With water spraying in all directions, it was gone. And so were the Klutz's glasses. They slid after the fish with a splash.

I took a quick look at her face. She was one sorry mess. But then she glanced at me. Through the wisps of her hair I saw her eyes. The brightest blue. She winked straight at me. She wasn't such a mess after all.

But I had no time for that.

I tried to uncrease Max's forehead with one finger. "Should I carry you?" I asked, "or will you walk?"

He took a step off my lap and headed along the sidewalk. "You know where you're going," I said. "You knew it all along."

I shouldn't have opened my mouth. Max stopped at the next pier and sat down on the curb. He didn't pay a bit of attention to a gull who was screaming at him. Instead he began to wash his front paw. He scrubbed and rubbed. Then he took a look at his claws. He still wasn't satisfied.

He began to work on the pads underneath.

I could feel my shirt sticking to my back. "You're stalling for time," I said. I scooped him up and headed for the next pier. And there we were at the corner garage. Trucks were all over the place. Panel trucks, front loaders, and a couple of flatbeds.

Max's claws dug into my shoulder.

"Come on," I said. "It's daytime. We'll just take a look. We can always scoot ourselves out of here."

And then I saw it. *Lumber Jack* on the side. "Same color," I told Max. "Same flag. Same truck."

Max closed his eyes.

A man was coming out of the garage with a pail of soapy water. JACK was tattooed in blue on one arm. A red heart was tattooed on the other. I almost began to run. I didn't want to give Max back, not to a guy who used his skin for a coloring book.

Max must have felt the same way. He plastered himself against my shirt.

I didn't run. I planted both feet on the path.

The man looked up. He didn't look bad, not like a killer. But who knew what a killer looked like anyway?

"Your cat?" I tried to sound as if I didn't care.

The man began to wash the truck with huge swipes of the brush. "I have a German shepherd," he said. "He'd eat that guy for lunch."

"He wasn't on your truck?"

The man looked at Max. "On my truck? He'd fly off the back so fast he'd think he was a jet."

I opened my mouth to explain. But it was too hot. I pushed my bangs off my forehead. "Who'd know where this cat belongs?"

"Maybe that kid, about your age. He hangs out in a wreck of a boathouse." Jack pointed with a soapy hand. "Calls it a club. Some club."

I looked toward the end pier. Underneath there were rocks and a boathouse. The man was right. It was a wreck. Gray boards were nailed together at a crazy angle. You'd have to stoop to get inside the door from this side. It would be easier to come in on the water side with a boat.

But the Crab's Legs was blocks away. I'd die of the heat before I walked back there to get it. I nodded at the man, "Thanks," and started down the driveway. I stopped. "Are you missing anything?"

"Missing a million dollars. Missing a boat that would sail me right out of the bay. Missing . . ."

"An amber ring?"

He didn't answer. He dipped the brush into the water and slopped it onto the hood of the truck, thinking. "Not me," he said at last.

I nodded. Then Max and I crossed to the pier side. We scrambled down along the rocks. "Stop. I have to get my breath," I told Max.

16

The rocks were sharp. "Not so great for sitting," I said, inching down on the edge of one. I reached into my pocket to check on the amber ring. It looked like one of those orange Tootsie Pops with the thin brown lines running through the amber.

I knew why. Mrs. Vorr, our best customer, had told me. Amber was sap from trees, she had said. Thick. Sticky. Things got trapped in it, pine leaves, bugs. Then the amber hardened and the stuff stayed there forever.

I sat there turning the ring in my hand. But Max was in a hurry. I slipped it back into my pocket and wiggled my way under the pier to the club. "Hey." I gave the door a bang with my fist.

No answer. Nothing. I picked Max up before I tried the door. It creaked open halfway. It was so dark inside I couldn't see. But Max could. He dug his claws into my shirt. Then, using my shoulder for a diving board, he leaped back over the rocks, away from the pier. And then he was gone.

I didn't have time to look in the club. I had to go after him. I reached out, ready to close the door. Just in that second, I knew someone was on the other side of me.

I heard the squeak of sneakers. I felt a hand on my back, pushing, pushing. . . .

And then I was inside the club, head first, skinning my knees on the dirt floor, the door scraping shut.

I was locked in.

5

COP

For a moment, I couldn't breathe. But then I remembered I was a detective. I rolled over toward the thin line of light at the bottom of the door. With one eye I could see the toe of a sneaker. It was on the skinniest leg I had ever seen.

"Let me out, you," I shouted.

The sneaker didn't stop. In a flash it took itself and its skinny leg over another rock.

I shoved at the door with both hands. It didn't budge. I sat up with my back against the wall. I put my feet up against the door and kicked as hard as I could.

No good. I could feel a spiderweb brush against my face. I shivered even though it must have been a hundred degrees. I was going to cry. I was going to faint. I was going to be in there forever. Orlando and I always stuck together. He'd be so worried. And what about Max?

I could hear him meowing. I could see one tiny black paw scratching under the door.

"It's no use," I told him. I reached out and touched a bit of his soft fur.

And then there was another voice. A high squeaking, "Look out, cat."

Something came barreling across the rocks and hit the door. It banged open and slammed against the side of the clubhouse wall.

The thing landed on me. The thing?

"I think I skinned my knees again," said the Klutz.

I didn't answer. I was embarrassed. All the time I had been pushing the door the wrong way. Some detective.

"What a place to lock yourself in," said the Klutz.

"I didn't." I wiped my eyes with the back of my hand before she could see the tears. "It was a maniac, a skinny maniac."

"The kid," said the Klutz. And then, "Could we get out of here? I'm allergic to spiders. I'm allergic to the dark."

We dragged ourselves outside to sit on the rocks. Max climbed on my lap and began to wash my face with his rough little tongue. I gave him a squeeze, then I dipped my feet in the bay, feeling the seaweed drift around my toes.

The Klutz yanked off her sneakers. Striped nail polish, I noticed. Neat. I wondered if she could see my eyes were red.

"Sometimes," she said just then, "the dark makes my eyes water."

I smiled a little and sniffled.

"Where do you live anyway?" the Klutz asked.

I pointed. "In back of the restaurant."

The Klutz nodded. "The one with the guy? Black mustache, white teeth. Cooks with peaches."

"My older brother. Exactly. His name is Orlando."

"Nice," she said.

"Mmm." I was thinking about something else. "You're all over the place," I began and broke off. "How can you see without your glasses?"

The Klutz raised her hands in the air. "You've got me. Great detective work."

"I'm in the business." Not exactly the truth. Not exactly a lie. "I'm on my first case," I told her quickly.

She leaned forward. "Katherine Kirov." She smiled. "My friends call me Kitty. I'm a patrolwoman. Sixty-first Precinct."

I was thrilled. I had spotted a cop.

"The glasses were fake." Kitty reached up and yanked. "So is the wig. I have a million of them. All disguises."

She looked like a different person. Gorgeous. Bright blue eyes. Black curly hair tight to her head.

I sat up straight. I couldn't wait to hear about her case. She held up her hand. "Can't say a word."

"No, of course not," I said, disappointed.

She rested her purse on a rock. "Well, I guess."

I swallowed. "I won't tell anyone."

"It's the most embarrassing thing," she said. "Someone around here is a purse snatcher."

Great. That was a terrific case to work on.

She bit her lip. "Someone stole *my* purse with ten bucks and a blue billfold inside. I have to solve this myself when I'm off duty. If the other cops find out about it, I'll never hear the end of it."

I nodded. "And I'm trying to find out where this cat belongs."

The Klutz reached out. She tweaked one of his ears gently. "Looks like he belongs to you."

My eyes were tearing again. I thought of something else. The amber ring. I'd have to tell her about it. I reached into my pocket. It wasn't there. I slapped my shirt pockets. It wasn't anywhere.

6

KITCHEN

It was Monday night. The restaurant was closed. We were going to have a catfish party, Orlando and me. And Max, later on, but Orlando didn't know it.

Orlando was at the stove, slapping the fish into bread-crumbs and then into the pan. He was singing, making up the words as he went along. *"We're having a dozen catfish. Won't you come back, red-headed lady?"*

And I was thinking. Some detective agency I was. Instead of finding things, I was losing them. Where was that amber ring anyway? I took a look at my bedroom door. Max was tucked up in there, asleep, I hoped.

Orlando slid three catfish and a bunch of peach-fried potatoes onto my plate. "For my number one girl," he said.

"I thought it was the redhead."

Orlando speared catfish four, five, and six onto his own plate. He twitched his mustache, grinning at me. "You want to be a detective. Why don't you find her for me?"

I narrowed my eyes. Finding a girlfriend for Orlando was

certainly not detective business. "I'd need a reward," I told him. "Cash."

He looked serious, but he didn't say anything. I bit my lip. I knew we didn't have much money. We were lucky to keep the restaurant open. I tried not to think about what would happen if we didn't get more customers soon. Instead I slathered a piece of catfish with Orlando's home-made tartar sauce. Delicious. His best meal.

Max must have agreed. I could see a small black paw reaching out from under my bedroom door. I cleared my throat. I jumped up. "Right back," I said, and edged catfish seven and eight off the plate on the stove, while Orlando was shoveling peach fries into his mouth.

"Everything will be cold," he said.

But I was out of the kitchen and into my bedroom in a flash. Orlando didn't have time to say another word. Someone was rapping at the back window.

"Lucky for you," I told Max. I gave him a pat on the head. He didn't pay attention, of course. He was scarfing up the catfish.

I was back at the table a moment later. But now we had someone else looking for a meal. The biggest pest in Sharkfin Bay, Leo the Lazy, was at the window, his bald head shining in the light. Leo was too lazy to get a job. He just lay around on the beach or slouched on the pier. He never even went fishing. That was because he was too lazy to bait his own fishing hook, Orlando always said.

Orlando shook his head, no, at Leo. I knew he didn't mean it, and so did Leo. After a minute, Orlando slid catfish nine, ten, and eleven onto a napkin and handed them out the door. For ten minutes, we listened to Leo whining. He had no money. Every time he got some, someone stole it. All his relatives were coming from Europe to visit and what would they think about that?

Orlando rolled his eyes at me and closed the door as Leo shuffled down the alley, still muttering.

"He never stops complaining," I said.

"Shifty piece of work," Orlando said as he divided the last catfish in half for us.

I wondered what he'd say if he knew Max was eating catfish. I was feeling like a shifty piece of work myself. "I took some extra fish off the stove," I said.

"This is your place, too, Minnie. I love it when you eat." He swallowed the last of the catfish in one bite. "Especially my food."

I opened my mouth. I wanted to say, *Then how about I keep the cat?* But I knew it was no use. I waited while Orlando made two huge peach sundaes. And afterward I told him I'd clean up. "Catfish frying pan and everything."

I did more than clean up. While Orlando went outside to fish from the boat, I not only did the dishes, but I looked for the amber ring. I searched in every cabinet, which took almost an hour. There must have been a hundred dishes, most of them cracked, and a thousand cups.

I sat back on my heels. The dishes with the red roses were missing, and the cups that went with them. Horrible looking things, but at least they had no cracks. I wondered if Orlando had finally thrown them away. I reached back and pulled out an old pink vase. My mother's. I ran my hands over it and put it back again. I was glad Orlando hadn't thought of throwing that away.

Max and I began on my peanut of a room. That took about three minutes.

But in the end, it was a waste of time.

I still hadn't found the amber ring.

7

KIDNAP

The thermometer outside the kitchen had just hit ninety. Right now I was watching Orlando. He was shredding lettuce, slicing tomatoes, chopping radishes. I was toasting the bread cubes. It was almost time for lunch at the Catfish Cafe.

"Another hot day," I told him nicely. I was trying to put him in a good mood. I had to get out of the kitchen fast. I had a case to solve, and a real detective to solve it with. I grinned to myself. My detective agency might turn out better than I expected after all.

"It's a scorcher," he grumbled. "Don't forget the anchovies for the salad."

He had grumbled his way through the morning. The fish was bad, the ice was melting, the soda was too hot, the coffee too cold. He sounded just like Goldilocks and the Three Bears.

It was a good thing he didn't know who was asleep under his nose. Asleep in the pot cabinet. Asleep in the huge blue

28

mixing bowl after a lovely breakfast of warm milk and all the anchovies.

It was a good thing Orlando didn't know Max was still my cat. Mine and Orlando's. "I think we should skip the anchovies," I said.

He put his head to one side. "Maybe you're right."

I had to say that Orlando, cranky as he was, had done a neat thing. This morning he had handed me two dollars.

"For what?" I asked.

"For cash," he said. "I wish I had more time to do stuff with you. Take you fishing or to a baseball game."

"Thanks." I waved the dollars in front of me. "You're the best."

I certainly wasn't worried about fishing or a ball game. I didn't have time for any of that either. And right now I could hear a chair scraping out in front. We had a customer. Orlando peeked out the curtain. I knew he was hoping it was the redhead.

But no. He shook his head. "Go out and take the order please, Minnie," he said. "I have to finish up here."

"No, you," I told him.

His mustache quivered. "Who's running this kitchen?"

"You're not supposed to have a child working, you know," I said.

"As if you're working."

"You just told me to take the order."

He reached for a jar of relish. "It's Mrs. Vorr," he said.

29

"Of course, it's Mrs. Vorr. That's just what I need. She will talk me into the grave. All about that guy leaving this summer." He snapped his fingers.

"Misha," I said and closed my eyes. Mrs. Vorr. I'd never get out of that restaurant today. The Klutz would never see me again.

"I thought you wanted me to finish the salad," I said. "And I am. My special deluxe invention salad with bits of peaches."

I smiled to myself. I knew he'd love it.

He did. I could see him smiling. And I had to say it, Orlando looked terrific with those great white Chiclet teeth. It didn't make any difference though. He pointed with one thumb and I was outside heading for Mrs. Vorr's table.

Mrs. Vorr had a swirl of gray-black hair. She had an amber necklace heavy enough to sink a ship. She had two amber bracelets and yes, two amber rings.

Her mouth was already open showing amber-colored teeth. "Darling little Minnie," she said.

In spite of all that talking, all that going on about how her darling Misha had left her, I liked Mrs. Vorr. There was a twinkle in her eye and she had a nice ha-ha laugh. But she wasn't laughing now. I tried to cheer her up.

"We have a darling little salad today," I told her. "A surprise salad." Mrs. Vorr loved to eat. If I had told her we had fried table leg her mouth would have watered.

Mrs. Vorr looked happy for a moment, but then she sighed. "I was robbed last night," she said. "Burglarized. Taken."

Orlando appeared with a frosty glass of iced tea on a tray. "Robbed?"

"My purse," she said. "With a million . . ."

"Dollars?" I asked.

Mrs. Vorr blinked.

Orlando frowned at me. I knew what he was thinking. Mrs. Vorr probably didn't have as much money as I did with my two dollars.

"No money," she said. "My purse was stuffed with everything else." She waved one baggy arm. "My best handkerchief. A token for the subway. A million pennies. But worst of all, a picture of Misha."

The purse snatcher had snatched again. I couldn't believe it.

Mrs. Vorr waved the other baggy arm. "My only picture of Misha. I used to think he left because he hated the apartment." She stopped waving and patted my hand. "There were dog hairs from poor dead Scotty all over the place." She rolled her eyes. "But now with everything else going on, I wonder if he was kidnapped."

"What happened to Scotty?" I asked, thinking road pizza.

"I think you're needed in the kitchen," Orlando told me.

31

"Old age," Mrs. Vorr said. "Sixteen."

"Did you see who took your purse?" I asked. "Any clues?"

"I think . . ." Orlando began again.

But Mrs. Vorr was shaking her head. "I didn't see anything."

"What did the police—"

"Minnie," Orlando said. I could almost hear him gritting his teeth.

Mrs. Vorr kept shaking her head. "I didn't tell them. I was all the way down on pier three. It was too much to walk . . ."

I nodded. I couldn't wait to get out of there now. I had to tell the Klutz. It was probably the same guy, the same purse snatcher, as we detectives would say.

Another customer took a table. It was Malka, the Dunkin' Donuts lady. She was Orlando's second-best customer. She was wearing about a hundred pounds of amber.

Before Orlando could ask me to do something, I sped into the kitchen. "Salad's all tossed, crisp and ready," I called.

I grabbed Max out of the mixing bowl. I was out the back door in three quick moves.

I was on my way to the Sixty-first Precinct.

8

CREEP

I walked a long way before I finally saw the orange-brown bricks of the station house. I took a deep breath and stopped at the corner. A blue-and-white patrol car was parked out in front, and a cop was heading up the sidewalk toward the double doors.

I wondered what a bunch of cops would say to my walking in there, worse yet with a black cat two steps in back of me.

I wondered what the Klutz would say.

I did it anyway. It was an emergency after all. "Come on, Max," I said, hoisting him up on my shoulder.

Inside I spotted a guy sitting behind a little cutout in the wall. "Yes, ma'am, can I help you?" He winked at me. "Or maybe your partner?"

"Who . . ." I began. He meant the cat. Funny. I wasn't used to being called ma'am either. It was nice, even though I knew he was teasing me. "I'm looking for . . ." I almost said the Klutz. I remembered just in time. "Officer Kitty . . ." I tried to remember the rest of it.

The guy winked at me again. "Coming right up," he said and shouted into a mike for her. "Police Officer Kirov, contact the office clerk."

The Klutz was there a minute later, not looking at all like a cop. She had a sweatband around her forehead, she was wearing shorts, and she looked as if she had spent the morning in the jungle. She was soaking wet. "Gotta keep fit," she told me. "We have a gym upstairs."

"Gotta tell you something," I said back. I jerked my chin at the other cop. "Privately."

He winked for the third time. He looked as if he had a tic with all that eye opening and closing.

"Come on," she said, "I'll show you the muster room."

I followed her across the hall. "We have roll call here on every shift," she said. "The sergeant tells us what crimes have been committed." She leaned forward. "Except my purse being taken. No one knows that except you and me." Now *she* was winking.

I tried a wink myself.

After all, I had just decided. I was definitely going to be a cop, definitely going to work in this precinct, definitely going to be hanging out in the muster room.

I began to tell Kitty about Mrs. Vorr. I remembered to whisper. At the same time I was looking around at the

pictures on the wall. Killers probably. Kidnappers.

The Klutz was listening to everything I had to say. She was listening so hard she leaned on a table and knocked over a set of dominoes. "We play sometimes after work," she said.

I bent down to help her pick them up. Max spent a few minutes batting a domino under the table. At the same time I was talking, finishing up about Mrs. Vorr. And the Klutz was nodding, her blue eyes squinched together.

Then we looked at the pictures together. "Creeps." She pointed to one. "This one's a car thief." She pointed to another. "This one sets fires." She nodded. "Don't worry. We get them sooner or later."

I tried to see if there was anyone I knew on the wall. No one. But then I moved closer, and so did Max. Someone up in the right-hand corner. Lots of hair, lots of eyebrows, a beard. One whole face of hair. There was something . . .

"He's a robber," the Klutz said. "Takes anything that isn't nailed down. She grinned at me. "He'd take a hot stove."

"What?" And then I got it. Who'd steal a stove that was still hot? A joke.

I looked at his face again. There really was something about him. . . .

"Do you think you know him?" Kitty asked. "We haven't seen him around in a long time."

I shook my head. "I guess not. I think it's just because he looks like a creep. Besides, I don't know who the purse snatcher is. I don't have any idea."

The Klutz knocked the domino set off the table again. "Neither do I," she said. "But I can tell you, I'm going to find out."

I squared my shoulders. "So am I."

9

CRAB'S LEGS

It was the next day, sticky and hazy. I knew the Klutz was off duty. But sooner or later she'd be looking for the purse snatcher. I tried to figure out what we'd do in the meantime, Max and me.

I could go around asking people if they knew who had lost a cat. But no, I'd do that tomorrow. Every time I thought about it, I felt a pain in my stomach and a lump in my throat.

Max meowed once and crossed the street to the pier. I followed him. I was thinking maybe we'd take a dip over at Minnow Beach. But *The Crab's Legs* was tied up in front of me. It was rolling gently in the water. And that's where Max was heading. An afternoon in the boat wouldn't be such a bad idea. But what about my detective agency? What about the amber ring?

I closed my eyes. Could I have left the ring in the kid's club? Could it have fallen out of my pocket on the rocks?

Max was already sitting in the bow of *The Crab's Legs*. It

would be easy to row over there. I'd watch to be sure the killer kid wasn't around. I'd sneak into the club. Yes, that's exactly what we were going to do. "Wait here," I told Max. "Don't move a muscle. I'll grab a flashlight."

The bay was kicking up a few waves by the time we got started. But the current was with us. I could feel the pull of it. I barely had to row. I sat there, my feet in a puddle of water, and enjoyed the ride.

The Crab's Legs was a little leaky. Not only that, but I saw that someone had been using it. There were puddles on the seat in the stern, and a piece of leftover hot dog. What nerve. Orlando and I took such good care of that boat. We loved it. We loved the bay and waving at the people along the piers. We loved watching them fish, watching . . .

. . . the Klutz. There she was, walking along the avenue with a purse on her arm. Her hair was stringy gray. She was bent over and she looked old, as old as Mrs. Vorr.

In an instant I knew what she was doing. She was playing decoy. I had seen stuff like that on television. A robber would come along, try to grab her purse, and bam, caught, into the slammer as they say.

I stopped pulling on the oars. I thought about docking at the next pier. I'd follow along to see what happened. But Max was staring at me, frowning.

"You don't think so?" I asked him.

He almost shook his head.

And the Klutz was turning down one of the side streets

39

anyway. I put my back into rowing again. I could see Leo the Lazy leaning against the pier, yawning. I waved at him. He didn't wave back. Of course not. It was too much work. I looked at him again. He was wearing a tie. A fat striped tie over his white undershirt. I grinned to myself. He was sprucing up for his family's visit from Europe. Some spruce-up.

A few minutes later, I could see the boards of the boathouse—I mean the club—sticking out over the bay. At first I didn't pull in. I pretended to be staring down at the green-brown water. I watched an empty soda can float by. I watched *The Black Dog* chugging along toward open water. And then, great luck, I saw the killer kid. No one else could have skinny legs like that.

The greatest part of the luck was that he was nowhere near the club. He was going around the side of Mrs. Vorr's apartment house, looking over his shoulder. What a sneak.

I wasn't rowing. The current was beginning to pull me out after *The Black Dog*, and the puddle was sloshing under my feet. But that was all right. I knew my way around the water. Maybe the kid was the purse snatcher. Maybe the kid had the amber ring. Suppose I didn't bother with the club? Suppose I followed him?

But it was the perfect time to search the club. I knew where the kid was. I thought about his pushing me. Don't worry, I told myself. He'd never get back in time.

"Yes," I told Max. "Let's see what's in there."

I angled *The Crab's Legs* along the rocks. I yanked on the big doors of the boathouse until one screeched halfway open. It was just enough. With a dip of the oars, I floated us gently inside. I looped the rope over the piling and switched on the flashlight. Then Max and I hopped out.

The door was on the opposite side. I could see the same streak of light underneath. The club itself was long enough for a boat and the rest of the stuff that went with it. I guessed that years ago someone had kept his fishing rod and reel there, and maybe an extra anchor and a coil of rope.

But now there was nothing. I ran the flashlight over every inch of that place. And Max ran his shiny white whiskers over every corner. The place was bare.

There wasn't an amber ring. Definitely not.

"If I had a club like this," I told Max, "I'd keep a pile of books in one corner. I'd have a blanket for cold gray afternoons. I'd have a box of Orlando's homemade peach nut cookies."

I wasn't watching the time. Suddenly I saw Max look up. I heard someone skittering along the rocks toward us.

I was in the boat in two seconds. And so was Max. I grabbed the oars and pushed. I pushed so hard the boat shot out of the club and into the bay. I looked back. I could hear my heart beating.

I couldn't see anyone, but someone was there. I knew Max was afraid. He was padding back and forth across the little seat in the bow. I swallowed. I was afraid. Some detective.

Instead I rowed back toward our pier. The current was strong against us now, and I had to row hard. I could see Lumber Jack up on the middle pier, and he saw me. He didn't wave, so I didn't wave either. I frowned. If I had dropped the amber ring on the rocks, he might have seen it. He might have come across the street and . . .

I shook my head. Maybe. But maybe not.

I wondered where Kitty the Klutz had gotten herself to by now. She was searching for a grown-up purse snatcher. But I was sure it was a kid. I began to trim my thumbnail with my teeth. "The only thing is," I told Max, "I didn't actually see the kid."

Had I been in the club long enough for the kid to get back? Suppose it hadn't been the kid? Suppose it had been someone else.

That's when the idea came to me. The scariest idea I had ever had.

I, Minnie, could be a decoy.

10

CASH

It was the next morning. Max was still in my closet asleep. But nothing else was left in there. I had pulled out all my clothes, my shoes, a winter hat, and every purse I had ever owned since I was four years old.

I was looking for a disguise.

I tried on everything. A skirt with a sweater. I'd die of the heat. A bathing suit over yellow tights. I looked like a clown.

I finally settled on black shorts, a black top, a straw hat that covered half my face, and a purse.

Not just any purse.

This one was a beauty. Big and red with patent leather loops. I had mined it up from Mrs. Vorr's garbage can a couple of weeks ago when I had the Mining for Gold Business.

I stuffed a bunch of toilet paper in the bottom of the purse to make it seem full. I tossed my two cash dollars from Orlando on top where anyone could see them. And then I was ready. Almost. I rooted around for a pair of sunglasses. Huge sunglasses that slid down my nose like the Klutz's.

I grinned at myself in the mirror. Out of the corner of my eye I could see Max stretching. "You can't come," I told him. "It's impossible. You'd give the whole thing away." I looked at him. "I'll get you an eggnog. Just don't let Orlando see you."

Max was stalking back and forth by now. To the door. To the window. I slipped into the kitchen to find some breakfast for him. I stood on tiptoe peering out behind the curtain. Orlando was across the street buying fresh porgies from the side of Captain Ed's boat. And Leo the Lazy was there looking for a free fresh fish. I had just a moment to get out of there.

I dropped a lump of tuna fish, two chicken slices, and a peach into a soup bowl. I cracked an egg on top and added half a glass of milk. Yuck, but Max would love it. All that stuff was good for him. I opened my bedroom door a little, slid in the bowl, and closed the door again as fast as I could.

Max meowed at me. A furious meow.

"You've got to hang out here," I said. "I'll be back as soon as I can."

I swallowed. What would I do if he made noise while I was gone? What would I do if Orlando found him in there? "Please be quiet, Max," I whispered.

The front door to the restaurant opened and closed.

Orlando was back. "Minnie," he yelled. "How about some breakfast?"

I tiptoed down the hall. "Ate already," I called. It was true. I had fixed myself a huge mess of leftover walnut ziti from last night. "I'm going out." I was out the door, across the street, and heading up the avenue before he could think of something else for me to do.

I bent myself over. I wanted to look old. I wanted to look helpless. I felt like an idiot. People were all over the place, buying newspapers, leaning against the pier, threading bait onto their fishhooks. Maybe I should go back, I thought. I was worried about Max. And Orlando might be looking for me any minute.

And then I thought about the Klutz. I thought about finding the purse snatcher. She'd be thrilled.

I walked a little farther. I straightened up to make a quick stop at Dunkin' Donuts. As Malka handed me a custard doughnut and a Coke, an amber bracelet clanked around her wrist. She saw me looking at it. "I wish . . ." she broke off. "I'd kill for amber."

I looked up quickly. "Really?"

She smiled, but before either one of us could say anything else, Malka was helping another customer. What did she mean? I wondered. Would she snatch purses for money to buy another piece? Or maybe she was just joking. Trying to figure out this stuff was great. I loved having a detective agency.

46

I watched her, wondering how she could hold up her head with the three amber necklaces around her neck.

"Great mashed potatoes at the Catfish Cafe yesterday," she said over her shoulder. "Crunchy, you know? What was in them?"

"Peaches," I told her. Walnut shells, I told myself. I went out the door and bent myself over again. I had only one dollar left, but it was worth it. I draped it on top and scurried over to the pier side of the street, taking an enormous bite of the doughnut and three quick gulps of soda.

I was watching ahead of me very carefully. There wasn't one killer type on the whole avenue.

If no one was around, why was I so uneasy?

I walked another block.

And that's when the purse snatcher snatched.

11

CATNAP

He grabbed the purse so hard, I was knocked off my feet. Both knees hit the cement. I was trying to get a look at him. At the same time, I was trying to hold onto the purse.

But he was too strong for me. Too strong for the purse. My arm twisted back. I could feel the loop snap. "Help, murder!" I yelled.

But it was too late. He was gone.

Next to me a fisherman scratched his head. "You two playing games?" he asked as he helped me up. "Pretty rough, if you ask me."

I dusted myself off. "I'm all right," I told him, but he had turned back to his fishing.

I turned to see if the purse snatcher was still on the pier. Of course not. But I knew who it was. I had a date with a purse snatcher, I told myself. All the detectives on television said that kind of stuff.

I headed straight for the club. The club door was open

and so were the water doors on the other side. It was light inside. And there he was, just sitting back against the wall relaxing his bones: the killer kid, with Mrs. Vorr's purse . . . and probably the amber ring.

"Hey, *you*." I took a good look at him. He was long and skinny like a stretched-out piece of bubble gum.

"Hey, *you*," he said. "Taking purses from old ladies." He picked up a stone and tossed it into the water.

"What?" I stared at my purse in his hands. Excuse me, Mrs. Vorr's garbage-can purse. I grabbed my last dollar out of the top.

"You're in big trouble." The kid aimed another stone at the bay.

"And you're headed for jail," I said. "As soon as I see my friend, my *cop* friend, you're in handcuffs. Tin bracelets as we say in the business."

The kid snorted. "I know a cop, too." Then he moved over.

I could see what he was doing, even though I couldn't believe it. He was making room for me to sit next to him.

My feet were tired. It had been a long morning. I slid down against the wall and checked out my knee. Not bad, the bleeding had stopped. I could see the kid out of the corner of my eye. If he tried one thing I'd be out of there fast, screaming for the Klutz.

He didn't try anything. "I'm sorry," he said, "really sorry. I didn't mean to make you fall."

"All right." I knew I sounded as grumpy as Orlando did sometimes.

We sat there listening to the water swish against the rocks, listening to the putt-putt of a motorboat in the bay. The kid didn't say anything else. He just sat there holding onto the purse, and waiting.

Waiting for what?

All that silence and throwing stones were beginning to get on my nerves. I cleared my throat.

Plop plop went two more stones. The kid still didn't say anything.

I tried to think of something else. I should have said, *How come you pushed me in here the other day? How come you stole my purse, and my money?* But I waited.

Then at last he opened his mouth. "Are you going to tell me about this?" He wiggled the purse with a couple of dirty fingers.

"It's my purse," I said. "You have to know that. You took it right off my arm."

"It's Mrs. Vorr's purse," he said.

I took a breath. "I took it out of her garbage can."

The kid started to laugh. "That's disgusting."

"It was perfectly good," I said. "Lots of compartments with zippers. Great color."

"Out of the garbage with bits and pieces of fish guts and orange peels?" He was laughing now.

"No, of course not," I said. "It was clean garbage." And then I was laughing with him. This kid had a neat face, a nice face. How could he be a killer? How could he have pushed me and knocked me down and stolen a bunch of purses?

"Mrs. Vorr is my friend," he said.

"You're some friend," I told him, picking up a stone. I shot it an inch farther than his.

"I'd never take anything of hers," he said. "I'd never take anything, period."

Then I did ask him. "Why did you push me the other day?"

"Mistake," he said. "I thought you were the one who had stolen my fishing gear."

I blinked. "This isn't just a purse snatcher," I said. "It's an everything snatcher. And he's snatching from everyone."

He nodded.

"I guess you didn't steal an amber ring," I said.

"What's—"

"Orange stone," I told him.

"I know." He wiggled his fingers. "The everything snatcher."

"Yes." I sat back. I thought about the whole thing. The ring on the truck. The cat on the truck. The Klutz's purse. Mrs. Vorr's purse, not the red one but another one. Round in circles. Back to the ring on the truck. How had it gotten there? Maybe Lumber Jack had stolen it, hidden it there, and then Max had come along. Maybe.

But the kid was talking now. A whole stream of talking. He was telling me about his two older sisters, his two younger brothers, telling me they had just moved to Sharkfin Bay. And he was asking me about my family.

"My family is Orlando," I said. "He taught me to read, to fish, to . . ." I tried to think of how to tell him Orlando was like my father and my mother.

I opened my mouth, but then I saw something. A row-boat. While we were sitting there, a light mist had come up over the bay. Everything seemed farther away. The boat looked like *The Crab's Legs* though. And someone was rowing it toward the boats moored out near the open water. A white wake shot up in back of the boat.

I stood up. "That's my boat." I couldn't see who was rowing. I could see only the head and shoulders bent over the oars.

And then I felt as if my heart was turning over. In the stern of the boat was a cat. "I think . . ." I began and swallowed. "It's my boat," I said again. "My cat."

The kid stood up. "I have a boat," he said. "We could follow him."

"Hurry," I said. "Please hurry."

12

CASMIR

We hopped into the kid's boat, a mess of a thing with dried fish guts all over the place, that he called *The Comet*. I could see Max in the stern of *The Crab's Legs*. He had one paw out over the edge of the boat. I knew he was crying, even though I couldn't hear him. I knew he was thinking about jumping into the water. No ordinary cat would do that, I told myself. But Max was no ordinary cat.

I knew something else. If I ever got him back, I'd never let him go again. Somehow Max and I had to stay together. And somehow I'd have to make Orlando understand. If he didn't, Max and I would freeze under the pier together next winter.

I was crying now. *Don't jump, Max,* I kept saying in my mind. *I'm coming to get you.* If only he'd turn around and see me. If only he knew I was there.

We were halfway across the bay now. The kid was rowing hard. "What's your name?" he asked, puffing a little.

I could just about talk. "Minnie."

He grinned at me. "As in Minnie Mouse?" he asked.

"No, as in Minneapolis." I shrugged a little. "I was born there." My eyes were still on Max, still trying to figure out who was rowing my boat. "What's your name?" I asked.

He rolled his eyes. "Casmir. It's a family name."

I bit my lip. "Unusual." I had to smile, even though I was crying. It was certainly no better than Minnie.

"But everyone calls me Cash," he said.

We were circling around the boats that were moored in the deep water. Everything seemed softer in the mist. I couldn't believe we were cutting through the water, the waves whipping up, and ahead of us was a criminal. Not a kid criminal. A real one. Someone who'd steal anything. Purses. Wallets. Fishing gear. And even a cat.

Now the person was pulling up to a boat. A large boat. This wasn't just a dinky rowboat like ours. It had a deck and a cabin, and portholes on the sides. I opened my mouth to yell.

"Don't," the kid said. "Wait." He angled his boat so it slid in behind a large sailboat. We sat there watching. The man reached out for Max and grabbed him with one hand. Max raked the man's arm with his claws. It was a small rake—he was such a small cat—and it didn't do any good.

All the time I was thinking. Why did the man look familiar? With his hat pulled down over his eyes, and moving fast, I couldn't get a good look at him. But I knew who he was. Somehow I had seen him before. For a moment, I thought he was Lumber Jack. Then the picture on the station-house wall bounced into my head. *The creep.* But the creep had tons of hair. He had a beard. And this man didn't seem to have either.

Now the man reached for the boat's ladder, and looped *The Crab's Legs* rope around it. Then he climbed the ladder himself, holding Max by the scruff of his neck. In a moment they disappeared inside.

We rowed a little closer. The boat was an old one. It could have used a couple of buckets of paint. On the back was the name, *The Amber Cat,* except the *b* had peeled off.

"Now what?" Cash asked.

"Now we catch the purse snatcher. Somehow." I was kneeling up in the rowboat watching. "But most of all we get my cat."

"You stole that cat?" he asked.

"What are you talking about?" I was watching *The Amber Cat* as carefully as I could. The man was still below the deck. If we could just row over, loop up Cash's boat, we could climb up and . . . And what?

"That's not your cat," Cash said. "It's Mrs. Vorr's. That's Misha."

I looked up at him. I began to shake my head. "But Misha's an old man," I said. "He left home, or—"

"He was kidnapped. Even Mrs. Vorr said so."

I closed my eyes. I had a picture of Mrs. Vorr in my mind. She had said, *I thought Misha had left because he hated the*

56

apartment. Poor dead Scotty's hair was all over the place.

"Dog hairs," I said aloud. "No wonder he hated it." And then I shook my head. I bit my lip trying to think. Maybe someone *had* kidnapped Max—I mean Misha. Catnapped him. Maybe he had escaped from the kidnapper, jumped onto the truck . . .

It was just too hard to figure out. Why would someone like the everything snatcher want a cat?

I had a terrible feeling in my chest, and I kept wiping tears off my cheeks. Even if we saved Max, I'd have to give him back to Mrs. Vorr. Mrs. Vorr was kind. Max would have a good home there. I could even help Mrs. Vorr vacuum up the dog hairs. Max wasn't mine. *Wasn't mine.* I couldn't swallow.

I didn't care what happened to me now. I was going to save Max. I was going to get that criminal for the Klutz. And then . . . I didn't know what would happen then.

Cash was still talking. He was acting as if I wasn't drowning in tears. "You think that guy has been stealing all that stuff?" he was saying. "What a shifty character."

I blinked. Someone else had said just that. *What a shifty character.*

But who? And when?

And then I had it. "I know who it is," I told the kid. "I know exactly who it is."

13

CABIN CRUISER

It was what Orlando had said in the kitchen at our catfish feast. *What a shifty character.*

"It's Leo the lazy," I said.

"Not so lazy after all," Cash said.

"No," I said. "While he was hanging out all over the place, he was watching, waiting for his chance to steal things. And no one would have guessed in a million years."

But now I knew. If only I could see the Klutz on the piers. I kept watching, but she was nowhere in sight. "Row over there," I told Cash, "over to his cruiser, *The Amber Cat.*"

"I think you're crazy," he said.

"I'm going to get that cat no matter what." I swallowed. He dipped his oars into the water again.

"Just get me over to the ladder. Then row around the

other side and hide there. If Leo climbs down onto *The Crab's Legs* again, he won't see you."

Cash was nodding.

"If he tries to kill me, go for help."

"Kill you?" Cash said. "How about we go for help now? I know a great cop. She's a little messed up, but . . ."

I had to smile. The Klutz. Kitty.

"No time," I said in my best detective voice. "I don't know what he's going to do to Max."

A moment later, Cash's boat was bumping gently against the ladder of *The Amber Cat*. I wasn't afraid. Not yet anyway. I was furious. I didn't even know what I was going to do when I boarded the cruiser. I guess I thought I'd sneak down into the cabin, grab Max, slide back outside to *The Crab's Legs*, and we'd both be free. And as soon as I saw Kitty, I'd tell her about Leo, all about Leo.

Another thing. The creep. Why did that picture in the muster room of the station house keep popping into my head?

The creep with hair.

Leo without hair.

Wait a minute.

The same eyes. The same person.

Yes. Leo had shaved his head. Shaved his beard. Good grief. He had even shaved his eyebrows.

I reached up and grabbed *The Amber Cat*'s ladder. I was over the side in a second and tiptoeing across the deck. The door to the cabin was just beyond a pair of seats with cushions. Large seats. I ducked down in back of one to get my breath.

I was finding it hard to breathe, my heart was pounding, and on the other side of the door Max was meowing. No, Misha was meowing. Sadly. Pitifully. Max thought he had lost his best friend. I almost called down to him. Instead, I tried to think. What next?

Before I had time to decide, Leo was up, out the door, and on the deck with me. He strode past, one inch away from my sneaker, one inch away from me. I raised my head the tiniest bit to watch as he disappeared over the side, down the ladder, and into *The Crab's Legs.*

He had never even seen me.

Cash wasn't so lucky.

I heard Leo shout, "Hey, you. What are you doing here?"

I saw the kid's boat suddenly appear around the side of the stern. He was rowing as fast as he could away from Leo. I wondered if it would do any good. Leo was stronger and *The Crab's Legs* was light in the water, much better than Cash's *Comet.*

But the kid was smart. He zigzagged between two boats that were moored in the bay and disappeared in the mist. I couldn't tell if Leo had seen him, and a moment later, Leo was gone.

Then I reached out with both hands and opened the cabin door, and Max leaped into my arms. He was making

little sounds, growling purring sounds, and in between he was digging his head into my neck. And I was rubbing his back and his ears. "Oh Max," I said.

I looked past him and into the cabin. It was Leo's kitchen, his living room, his home. And I couldn't believe what I was seeing. Pieces of wood were piled in the corner with Lumber Jack's name printed on the ends. Orlando's plates with the red roses were stacked on one shelf. The amber ring swung gently on a hook in front of the porthole. A blue billfold lay in a half-opened drawer, and a fishing rod was on the floor.

I picked up a picture from a table. It was a picture of a cat. My cat, Max. Mrs. Vorr's cat, Misha.

"He decorated his whole boat with other people's things," I told Max. I remembered what the Klutz had said: *He'd take a hot stove.* His family, coming from Europe. He was sprucing everything up for them.

I backed out of the cabin and onto the deck. Max wasn't letting go of me. I could feel each one of his little claws in my arm. I looked across the bay, but I still couldn't see Leo, and I couldn't see Cash.

But I thought about something and my heart began to pound. Max and I had to get away from the boat before Leo came back.

14

KEY

I bit my lip. There was no way to get off *The Amber Cat*. I looked down at the water swirling around the cruiser. There was no *Crab's Legs* to row us ashore.

Suppose I dragged up the anchor? The cruiser would drift. We might get close enough to shore to call to a fisherman. I shook my head, no. It was still misty. It seemed as if the boats in the bay, the fishermen, and even the piers were disappearing in the gray light. And something else. We'd be moving with the current, and in a few minutes we'd be out of the bay into the ocean.

I saw a sea robin swimming just under the surface of the water. I was a good swimmer, even when the waves were rough, but the next boat was far. So was the shore. And I'd never leave Max.

Instead I cupped my hands around my mouth and began to call. There was no one close enough to hear, of course. After a moment, Max jumped out of my arms. Tail high, he started across the deck, looking back at me. I stopped yelling. I watched him. And then I saw it. A key, dangling from the motor. I swallowed. All I had to do was give the key a quick turn. I could picture the motor starting up. I could see myself turning the wheel, steering the boat.

I'd never done anything like that before. My hands were wet just thinking about it. I could start the cruiser easily enough. But what about the rest of it? Keeping us away from other boats, away from open water? And worse, how could I stop it?

I reached out anyway, taking the key in my cold fingers, and then I saw something else. A rowboat coming toward us. It was Leo, in *The Crab's Legs*, and he was close. Another few strokes and he'd be at the ladder.

I didn't stop to think. I scooped Max up, darted into the cabin and closed the door in back of us. There was really no place to hide in that small place. There was a porthole, though, just large enough for me to get through.

But I was on the other side of the ladder. There'd be no boat underneath, nothing but the water and all that mist. I heard Leo scrabbling around on the deck. A moment later he fumbled with the door. Against my chest, Max's heart was pounding harder than mine.

I took a breath and pulled the porthole window open. We scrambled out head first, and dived into the water below. I could hear the sound of it as we went under, a roar in my ears. I was choking. My mouth, and nose, and even my ears were filled with the sea. But all the time I was thinking *Max*, holding onto Max, I knew I'd never let him go.

And then I kicked hard, my head was up, and I was breathing. I was holding Max above me, and I thought I heard a voice. Not Leo's, it was Cash's. He was right there, nosing his fish-guts boat toward us. A moment later Max was over the side, safe again, and so was I.

I was shivering, but the sun was coming out. I could feel its warmth on my head. I looked down. In my hand, clutched so tightly it had left marks on my palm, was the key to *The Amber Cat*.

And Leo? We were around the side now. I couldn't see the porthole anymore, but I could see *The Crab's Legs* tied up against the ladder. Max shook himself off, spraying half the bay over my legs, and then I thought of something we could do.

I was still coughing, but I pointed, holding up the key. He was smart, that Casmir. He knew what I was thinking. With four strokes of the oars, he had us bumping up against *The Crab's Legs*. I hopped across into my boat and fumbled with the rope, trying to unloose it from the cruiser.

Leo burst out of the cabin as *The Crab's Legs'* rope slid away from the cruiser's ladder into the water. I pushed against the side of *The Amber Cat* with one oar and watched as slowly, slowly, the distance between the two boats widened.

15

CAUGHT

We kept looking back, Cash in his boat, and I in mine. Max was having a fit. He wanted to cross over to me, and I kept yelling for him to wait.

I was afraid Leo would do something. I was afraid he might even try to swim after us. He didn't, though. He was standing there, caught on the deck of *The Amber Cat* shaking his fist at us.

Cash and I nosed both rowboats into the club together and jumped out. I looped Max up around my neck like a collar. I could feel his fine white whiskers twitching. "We're safe now," I said.

The three of us headed up the rocks toward the pier and Emmons Avenue. I could see the big clock at the fishing station across the way. The Klutz would be on duty now, walking her beat or maybe driving one of the cars we always saw patrolling the streets.

"I think I saw your fishing rod," I told the kid. I shook

my head. "You should see all the stuff in there. The amber ring . . ."

The kid was nodding, listening. "The name of his boat, *The Amber Cat*. I bet he stole the amber ring . . ."

"Yes," I said, "and kidnapped the cat . . ."

The kid cut in. "They fit in with the boat."

We found the Klutz on Whitman Avenue. She was driving a blue-and-white patrol car. She pulled over to the side, smiling, as soon as she saw us. Cash and I leaned in the window, but Max hopped over us and onto her lap.

I have to say the Klutz looked terrific in her blue uniform. Her hat was tipped back over her own dark curly hair, her shirt ironed so carefully you could see the lines where she had folded it. Her silver shield was pinned to the front. She really looked like a cop.

But I didn't have time to tell her that. We had to tell her the whole Leo story, interrupting each other to get the words out. It almost looked as if Max was nodding with every sentence. She reached over and opened the back door of the patrol car, and a moment later, we were racing for the Sixty-first Precinct to call the harbor patrol for help.

The Klutz dropped us off at pier thirteen at the far end of the bay. "I know you'd like to come with me," she said, "especially Max." She gave his ear a small tweak. "But the next best thing is to stand right here. We'll be bringing Leo right to this pier on his way to the station house."

And so we stood there, Cash, Max, and me. It took a

long time. We watched about a dozen fishing boats come in and set up their tables to sell bonita and albacore tuna and striped bass. We watched them hose down the boats and sweep off the decks with wet brooms. The kid rooted around in his pocket and came up with enough money for two frozen fruit bars apiece.

And then at last, the sleek blue-and-white harbor boat came along with a couple of cops, Kitty, and Leo—"In tin bracelets," I told Cash.

"I was just going to say that," he told me. "I'm in the detective business. That's how I got to know Kitty Kirov. I asked her for tips. How to start out. Stuff like that."

Neat, I wanted to tell him. We'd stick together on our next case. But I was too busy listening to Leo talking. He was talking to Kitty, talking to anyone who would listen.

"My cousins were coming, my uncles. My cruiser was bare," he said. "I had to take the stuff."

"An amber ring," I said. "And a cat."

"A fishing rod," Cash said.

The Klutz was nodding. "Wait until you see your jail cell," she told Leo. "Now that's really bare."

16

COOKING

It was a week later. It seemed like a party in the restaurant. It *was* a party, in honor of Igor, Mrs. Vorr's new cat. "You and Minnie will have to keep Misha," Mrs. Vorr had told Orlando. "He and Igor will never be happy together."

That was fine with Max and me. And even Orlando knew when to give in.

So Max had a new home. He moved into the restaurant in two seconds, letting us know the blue mixing bowl was his for naps, letting us know he needed the best pillow on my bed at night, letting us know he liked shrimp and anchovies and he detested potatoes and vegetables.

And right now, the restaurant tables were filled, just the way they had been all week. Maybe it was because everyone in Sharkfin Bay had heard about our capturing Leo the Lazy.

But I think there was another reason we were doing so well. After her eight-to-four tour of duty every afternoon, Kitty took over the kitchen.

Sometimes she dropped pots and pans, or spilled raspberry sauce and whipped cream. But in between she made *piroshki*, which were little meat turnovers that melted in your mouth, and *borscht*, an icy cold pink soup. For dessert there was *lodichka*, macaroons that looked like tiny chocolate boats, and *charlottka* which was the best jelly roll I had ever tasted.

The smells of those Russian dishes drifted out onto the piers, and no one could resist. Fishermen put down their rods to stand in line. Tourists hustled themselves in the door, and the phone jangled off the hook with people asking for reservations.

Everyone gave Max a pat at the front counter before they were seated. He was sitting there at the cash register, watching the action. He looked great wearing the amber-colored collar the cops in the Sixty-first Precinct had given him.

And Orlando hadn't stopped smiling once. After Kitty had taken Leo away, she had come back to treat us to dinner. We had told Orlando all about what had happened, the Klutz, the kid, and I.

"And so," I had finished up, "Leo took the cat, he took the amber ring, and he was taking wood. Straight off Lumber Jack's truck."

"Except," Cash said, "Jack came along and started the truck, and the cat jumped back on with the ring in his mouth."

I don't know if Orlando was paying that much attention

to the story. He hadn't taken his eyes off Kitty. Maybe it was because of her red wig.

It turned out that she was Orlando's redhead all along. And even I, the best detective in Sharkfin Bay, hadn't figured that out.

And right now, she winked as she passed me a plate of *blinchiki* to bring out to the front. She was wearing a great amber ring that Orlando had given her this morning. No, it wasn't *that* ring.

Right now I passed the plate to Malka from Dunkin' Donuts. She waved her pinkie finger with *the* amber ring. It was back where it belonged. "I never thought I'd see this again," she said. "I was wishing and wishing for it. And to think I had treated Leo the Lazy to a dozen vanilla crullers."

I kept going then, past the tables, out to the cash register. I scooped Max up, along with a couple of mints. We were heading out to the piers with Cash. We had to look for the next mystery to solve.

KITTY'S PEACH SURPRISE
(Max likes the crust; Minnie likes the whole thing)

6 slices of bread with the crusts cut off (Give the
crusts to the cat.)

6 slices of butter (About a stick. Save a bit to butter
the pan.)

6 tablespoons of brown sugar

6 fresh peach halves (Don't forget to peel them. Plant
the pits in the garden.)

Get a grown-up to help preheat the oven to 350 degrees.
Butter a 9 x 13 baking pan. Butter each slice of bread.
Sprinkle half the sugar on top. Put a peach half, cut side
down, in the middle of each slice. Sprinkle the rest of the
sugar on top of the peaches. Bake for fifteen minutes.

What's the surprise?
Orlando says it's a sprinkle of cinnamon.
Minnie says it's a spoonful of whipped cream.
Kitty Kirov says it's a scoop of peach ice cream.